H. CH. ANDERSEN
THUMBELINA

RETOLD AND ADAPTED FOR THE ILLUSTRATED VERSION
by GABRIELA MORARU

ROYDON PUBLISHING CO LTD   81 Goswell Road — London E.C.1

nce upon a time there was a woman yearned after a little child, but she did not know where to get one from. So she went to an old witch, and said: "My deep-felt wish is to have a little child. Could you tell me where to get one from?" "Oh! that is easy", answered the old witch. "Here you have a barleycorn; but mind you! it is not the kind which grows in the field, and which chicken get for food. Put it in a flowerpot." "Thank you," said the woman, and gave the witch a few coins. Then she went home and planted the barleycorn. In the twinkling of an eye there grew up a beautiful flower, which looked like a tulip, but its petals were so closely tied together as though it were but a bud.

"What a lovely flower!" said the woman, and she kissed its yellow and red petals. Just as she did so the flower opened with a pop. It was a tulip indeed, but right in the middle of the flower there sat upon the green pistil a tiny girl, delicate and graceful to behold. She was not taller than a thumb, and for this very reason she was called Thumbelina.

A walnut shell stood for her cradle, blue violet petals were her mattress and a rose petal was her coverlet.

One night, as she lay comfortably in her little cradle, a Toad crept through the broken pane of a window. The Toad was ugly, swollen, and moist. "She would make a perfect wife to my son." thought the Toad, and she grabbed the walnut shell in which Thumbelina was sleeping, and hopped through the window back into the garden.

At the end of the garden flowed a river with swampy banks, and here dwelt the Toad with her frightful son. "Let us set her upon a water-lily leaf till we get the room under the marsh ready."

Early in the morning the little girl woke up, and when she saw where she was she began to cry bitterly. The large leaf upon which she sat was surrounded by water, and she could not reach the river bank at all. The Toad bowed low before her in the water and said: "Here is my son; you shall marry him and

live together down there in the marsh." "Croak! Croak!" was all
the son could say.

They took the little cradle, and swam away with it. Thumbelina
was left alone upon the large leaf, and she began to cry, even more
bitterly this time, for she did not want to live in the marsh, and

to marry the dreaded son of the Toad. The little fish swimming in the water lifted out their heads to see the girl and felt miserable at the thought that such a beauty was to live in the marsh. No, that must never happen! They clustered round the green stalk of the leaf and started to gnaw it with their teeth till the leaf broke off and ran down the river. Thumbelina got farther, and farther away, where the Toad could not reach her any more. She passed along many cities, and the birds on the trees chirped when they saw her: "What a lovely girl!"

A delicate white butterfly kept her company and landed on the leaf, as he liked Thumbelina very much. The girl was happy, as the Toad could no longer reach her and everything she saw around her filled her heart with joy. The sun shone upon the water and made it glitter like pure gold. Thumbelina unfastened her sash and tied one end of it to the butterfly and the other to the leaf.

As she was sailing, a big Cockchafer came flying; he grabbed her by her slender waist, and flew with her up into a tree. How scared poor Thumbelina was! But she was more distressed at the thought of that handsome white-winged butterfly. The other cock-chafers living in that tree came to pay her a visit and seemed quite disatisfied. The lady cockchafers declared her ugly, and so she was taken down and put on a daisy. Bitter tears filled her eyes as she imagined herself unattractive and dull.

All summer long Thumbelina stood by herself in the large wood, and had the honey of the flowers to eat and the morning dew to drink. Then, the long bleak winter came, and with it the chilly snow. Every snow-flake that fell upon her was like a shovelfull thrown upon any of us, as she is so short compared to us. What could she do? She wrapped herself in half a dry leaf, but still she was shivering and her teeth were chattering through the cold.

At the edge of the wood there stood a large corn field. The corn had been harvested long before, and only the dry stubble covered the frozen ground. To Thumbelina the stubble looked like a real wood. She set out through the stubble trembling and shivering, and after some time she came to the door of the Field Mouse, who made his dwelling there. Thumbelina stopped at the door like a beggar little girl, and asked for a tiny bit of corn, as she had not eaten for the last two days.

"Poor little creature," said the Field Mouse, who was rather kind-hearted, "come on in, and warm yourself up. Let us have dinner together!" As she enjoyed her company, she went on:

"You may stay here through the winter. In return you tidy up my house and tell me stories." Thumbelina did as she was told, and they had a good time together. One day, the Field Mouse said: "We have a guest today. One of my neighbours pays me a visit once a week. He is by far better off than I am. His house has many rooms, and he wears a splendid black coat. If you could only marry him! There is merely one inconvenience; he is blind. Tell him the most enchanting stories you know." But Thumbelina did not give it a thought. Their neighbour was a Mole, and she had no intention of marrying him.

The Mole came dressed up in his much-praised fur coat, and

Thumbelina had no other choice but to sing and tell him stories. The Mole fell in love with her because of her enthralling voice; but he said nothing as he was a cautious creature.

Not long ago he had dug an underground passage from his house to the Mouse's. The Mole invited Thumbelina and her old companion to take a walk in the passage whenever they wished. He also mentioned a dead bird that lay down there and which must not frighten them away. It was a Swallow, his wings pressed tightly against his body, his feet numb with cold and his head drawn under his feathers. The poor bird had certainly died of cold. The Mole thrust up his stumpy nose against the ceiling, and made a large hole so that the day-light could come down. Thumbelina was grieved at his sight, as she loved the birds who graced the summer with their song. The Mole, however, pushed the bird with his short legs.

Thumbelina said nothing, but when the Mole and the Mouse turned their backs she kissed the swallow upon his closed eyes.

At night, Thumbelina could not sleep. She got out of bed and wove a beautiful carpet of hay, which she carried to the bird and spread over him. Then she took some soft cotton from the Mouse's store room, and cloaked the swallow to keep him warm. The girl laid her cheek upon the bird's breast and shuddered. She heard the

bird's heart beating. The Swallow was not dead after all. He had only been numb, and now that he had been warmed up he came back to life.

The next night she crept to him again. The Swallow breathed life again, but he was terribly weak. For only an instant he could open his eyes and looked at Thumbelina. "Thank you dear little girl", said the weak swallow. "I feel wonderfully warm; I shall recover my strength again and be able to get out of here and fly in the warm sunshine." "Oh!" exclaimed the little girl, "it is so cold and there is so much snow out there. You better stay here and I shall look after you".

When spring came and the sun warmed up the earth, the Swallow bade Thumbelina farewell.

Their neighbour, the tedious black-furred Mole had proposed to her. But Thumbelina could show no joy, as the Mole was tiresome, and she simply could not stand him.

When autumn came, Thumbelina had everything ready for the wedding.

"The wedding is in a month", said the Mouse. As Thumbelina heard that she started to sob and nothing could stop her, as she did not want to marry the Mole. She grew more distressed since she had to part with the sun for ever. While she lived with the Mouse she could, at least, wink at it from the threshold.

"Farewell bright sun, farewell!" she cried. She embraced a little red flower and whispered: "Send my good wishes to the Swallow."

"Tweet, tweet!" she suddenly heard and up she looked. There was the Swallow. "Winter is coming," chirped the bird, "and I am leaving for the warm countries. Will you come with me?

I shall carry you on my back. Come, dear Thumbelina, you who have saved my life as I was lying underground." "I am coming," replied Thumbelina, and the Swallow took her on his back. The little girl spread her legs on the bird's wings, tied herself to one of the stronger feathers, and the Swallow flew up in the blue air, over woods and seas till they reached the sea-shore. There, among the fruit-laden trees stood a white marble palace of the olden times.

"That is my house," chirped the Swallow. "Fragrant flowers are growing everywhere. I shall put you on one of them and you may live there. The Swallow alighted and set the little girl on a petal. Oh, she could not believe her eyes! Right in the middle of the flower stood a little man, white and transparent as if glass-

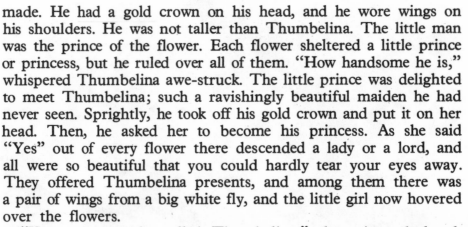

made. He had a gold crown on his head, and he wore wings on his shoulders. He was not taller than Thumbelina. The little man was the prince of the flower. Each flower sheltered a little prince or princess, but he ruled over all of them. "How handsome he is," whispered Thumbelina awe-struck. The little prince was delighted to meet Thumbelina; such a ravishingly beautiful maiden he had never seen. Sprightly, he took off his gold crown and put it on her head. Then, he asked her to become his princess. As she said "Yes" out of every flower there descended a lady or a lord, and all were so beautiful that you could hardly tear your eyes away. They offered Thumbelina presents, and among them there was a pair of wings from a big white fly, and the little girl now hovered over the flowers.

"You must not be called Thumbelina," the prince declared. "This is quite unbecoming for a girl so beautiful. We shall call you Maya."

"Farewell, farewell," sang the Swallow, and he flew back to Denmark. There he had a nest over the window of the man who can tell beautiful tales. And from him we learnt the whole story.